HOP
NTON, MA 02780

W9-CBL-517

HOPEWELL SCHOOL LIBRARY
TAUNTON, MA 02780

THE SNAIL HOUSE

For Solly
G.T.

And Kate.
A.A.

Text copyright © 2000 by Allan Ahlberg
Illustrations copyright © 2000 by Gillian Tyler

All rights reserved.

First U.S. edition 2001

Library of Congress Cataloging-in-Publication Data

Ahlberg, Allan.
The snail house / Allan Ahlberg ;
illustrated by Gillian Tyler.—1st ed.
p.   cm.
Summary: Grandma tells Michael, Hannah, and their baby
brother the story of three children who shrink to such
a small size that they decide to live in a snail's shell.
ISBN 0-7636-0711-8
I. Tyler, Gillian, ill. II. Title.
PZ7.A2688j Sn 2001
[E]—dc21   98-42389

10 9 8 7 6 5 4 3 2 1

Printed in Hong Kong

This book was typeset in Golden Cockerel.

The illustrations were done in
watercolor and pen and ink.

Candlewick Press
2067 Massachusetts Avenue
Cambridge, Massachusetts 02140

HOPEWELL SCHOOL LIBRARY
TAUNTON. MA 02780

ALLAN AHLBERG
THE SNAIL HOUSE

illustrated by
GILLIAN TYLER

CANDLEWICK PRESS
CAMBRIDGE, MASSACHUSETTS

E
Ahl
4-30-01
22510566

"Come here, children," Grandma said.
The children came.

"Gather round—climb up now."

And so they did, all warm and sweetly smelling from their strawberry picking, and into Grandma's lap.

"A story, Grandma?" Michael said.

"Story?" added Hannah.

"A story...yes," said Grandma.

"About the horses?" Michael said.

"Hozzes?" added Hannah.

"No—no hozzes this time, sweetheart." Grandma cuddled them up inside her mighty arms. "This time,"—she gazed across the dusty evening garden—"this time it's the turn . . . of something else."

"Once upon a long, long time ago there was a boy and his sister and their little baby brother who all of a sudden got so very, very small that they could leave that house of theirs by a crack under the door—and *no one notice*."

"My!" said Hannah.

"So one day that's just exactly what they did. They left that house, all on a bright and sunny morning, the dew still on the grass, and went to live, for a little while at least, in their own, their absolutely very own and private . . . snail house."

"Snail house?" cried Michael.

"Snail house—yes."

"On the back of a snail?"

"That's right. And it was a proper house too, with a door and windows, roof and chimney, table, chairs, three little beds, curtains, and crockery—everything!"

"It have a TV?" Hannah said.

"No TV, sweetheart, not in those days. But a radio, yes."

"So there they lived in that house, which, of course, was a *moving* house. And they kept it spotless clean; dusting the furniture, sweeping the floor, washing the windows. And they fed that snail friend of theirs as well, with bits of lettuce and such. And they read books, hung their washing on the line, minded the baby . . ."

"And had *adventures*," Michael said.

"And had adventures," Grandma said. "Three adventures, actually."

"One each," said Michael.

"Hm, sort of." Grandma leaned across to the baby in his stroller. His little cotton sun hat had slid down over his sleeping face. She moved the hat aside.

"The first adventure that those children had was . . . the *earthquake*. One minute they were having breakfast, the baby in his highchair, the sun shining, grasshoppers chirruping, radio on. Then, all of a sudden — wallop! — the whole snail house shook. Plates smashed, chairs fell over, and that poor old snail himself just wobbled like a jelly."

"It was a human being, I'll bet!" cried Michael. "Stamping around."

"Or pussycat," added Hannah.

"No—no person caused that sudden thump, nor pussycat neither. No, you'll just about never guess." Grandma waved a flitting moth away. "You see, what caused that earthquake was . . . an *apple*."

"Falling from a tree!" cried Michael.

"That's right. Bouncing down upon that orchard grass like a bomb, and missing the snail by inches."

"Then did they eat it?" Hannah asked.

"Well, some of it. It was pretty big for them, you see. Only then they shared it, sort of, with a young red fox who just that very moment came slipping through those orchard trees toward the river."

"After the ducks," said Michael.

"Hm." Grandma shuffled her load of children and made herself more comfortable on the wide veranda steps. Traffic hummed on the distant road, headlights faintly gleaming in the gathering dark.

"The second adventure that those children had was . . . the *disappearing baby*. He just crawled off one time, while his brother and sister were playing catch— for only a moment, it seemed—and was lost from sight in the forest of grass. Well, those children, once they realized what had happened, looked everywhere for that infant, ever more frantic and tearful too, till—lo and behold—they spotted him."

"Ah!" said Hannah.

"Yes, spotted him . . . halfway up a dandelion stalk. See, it was leaning over, not growing straight. *Next* thing, he was floating away, that baby, hanging on tight to one of those fluffy seeds."

"Like a parachute!" cried Michael.

"Hm . . . floating away . . . and floating." Grandma paused. Next door a phone was ringing.

"They catch him?" Hannah asked.

"By and by, oh yes, after much puffing and running and chasing, they caught him and carried him home."

"To the snail house," Michael said.

"The snail house," Grandma said.

"The third adventure, though, was the *scary* one." That phone again, and now a dog barking. "This began one evening right after a shower of rain, the drops like sacks of water exploding all around. The snail house was moving through the half-light and the dampness—conditions which a snail most loves—when . . . there was a heavy movement above . . . a shadow."

"The children felt it in their house and peeped out of the window."

"What they see?" said Hannah.

"I know," said Michael.

"They see . . . they saw, high above and all before them, advancing stately through the grass—a mighty giant bird."

"Oh!" cried Hannah.

"It was a thrush—a lovely singing bird, of course, but for a snail, you see —"

"Thrushes eat snails!" cried Michael.

"That's right. For a snail, I'm bound to say, a thrush was a *tiger* in that garden. And on it came on its beanpole legs, looking here and there with its dark eye —"

"They smash their shells on a rock!" cried Michael.

"No!" cried Hannah.

"Well, that poor old snail just tucked his head in and hoped. But the children, though, they grabbed some pots and pans and rushed outside, banging and clattering and hollering —"

"Scared it off!" cried Hannah.

"No, sweetie, not quite, though they were hugely brave to try. No, it was a sudden prowling cat did that. She was the tiger in the thrush's garden. Hm."

Just then another *actual* cat came brushing against them in the darkness on the veranda.

"Then up that thrush went flying into a tall tree, and off that cat went prowling some more—"

"Here's *your* cat, Grandma," Michael said.

"Monty, Monty," Hannah called.

"And, by and by, off and away on its ever shiny trail went the snail house, under the brightening stars, down at last, come midnight, to the very water's edge . . .

to watch the river flow."

The stroller squeaked. The baby
was stirring, his pale round face like
a luminous clock in the dark.

"Which is the end," said Grandma,
planting the children on the steps and
rising to her feet.

"Next day, having properly thanked
that snail for his house and hospitality,
they went back to their proper size . . .
and home."

In the kitchen Michael put on the light. Grandma — the slowly waking baby now in her arms — came following after. Out on the veranda Hannah was standing yet, gazing into the muffled blackness of the garden.

The cat was sitting on the top veranda
step, while over and beyond the invisible
hedge, horses were whinnying.

HOPEWELL SCHOOL LIBRARY
TAUNTON, MA 02780

E
AHL

Ahlberg, Allan.

The snail house.

E
AHL

HOPEWELL SCHOOL LIBRARY

The snail house.

22510566

DATE	BORROWER'S NAME	

HOPEWELL SCHOOL LIBRARY
TAUNTON, MA 02780

BAKER & TAYLOR